Herón Márquez

Lerner Publications Company
Minneapolis

This book is dedicated with great love and humor to my mother and father (Catalina and Luis), my nieces (Teresa, Crystal, Jessica, and Marisa), my nephews (Alex, Andrew, Diego, Jacob, Nathan, and Robert), my brothers (Jose, Raz, and Lalo), and my sisters (Juana, Tiggie, Martha, and Maria). Thanks for putting up with me.

A&E and **BIOGRAPHY** are trademarks of the A&E Television Networks, registered in the United States and other countries.

Some of the people profiled in this series have also been featured in A&E's acclaimed BIOGRAPHY series, which is available on videocassette from A&E Home Video. Call 1-800-423-1212 to order.

This book is available in two editions:
Library binding by Lerner Publications Company,
   a division of Lerner Publishing Group
Soft cover by First Avenue Editions,
   an imprint of Lerner Publishing Group
241 First Avenue North
Minneapolis, MN 55401 U.S.A.

Website address: www.lernerbooks.com

Library of Congress Cataloging-in-Publication Data

Márquez, Herón.
    Latin sensations / by Herón Márquez.
       p.   c.m — (A&E biography)
    Includes bibliographical references and index.
    Summary: Profiles five influential Latino entertainers of the 1990s, Ricky Martin, Selena, Jennifer Lopez, Enrique Iglesias, and Marc Anthony, detailing their rise to stardom and their effects on the American music scene.
    ISBN 0-8225-4993-X (lib. bdg. : alk. paper)
    ISBN 0-8225-9695-4 (pbk. : alk. paper)
    1. Selena, 1971–1995—Juvenile literature. 2. Martin, Ricky—Juvenile literature. 3. Lopez, Jennifer, 1970– —Juvenile literature 4. Anthony, Marc—Juvenile literature. 5. Iglesias, Enrique, vocalist—Juvenile literature. 6. Singers—Latin America—Biography—Juvenile literature.
    [1. Singers. 2. Hispanic Americans—Biography.] I. Title. II. Series.
    ML400.M339 2001
    782.42164'092'368073—dc21   00-008876

Manufactured in the United States of America
1 2 3 4 5 6 – JR – 06 05 04 03 02 01

CONTENTS

In July 1999, Ricky Martin appeared in Paris, France, to promote his new album, Ricky Martin. Security guards had to protect Ricky from throngs of screaming fans.

INTRODUCTION

The world went crazy in 1999. Not literally, of course. But along with the usual wars, natural disasters, economic crises, and the dawn of a new millennium, a handsome, hip-swiveling Latino singer took the world by storm that year. His name was Ricky Martin.

Already a superstar in Latin America and Europe, where he had sold millions of albums, Martin exploded onto the U.S. entertainment scene in 1999. At the Grammy Awards in February, he delivered a sizzling performance. By summer, his catchy tune "Livin' la Vida Loca" (Livin' the Crazy Life) had become the number-one song in the country. Martin seemed to be everywhere: on radio, television, and the Internet. His face was splashed across the covers of dozens of entertainment magazines, as well as news magazines such as *Time* and *Newsweek*. All of a sudden, it seemed, Martin was not just *new*, but *news*.

Not only did Martin capture the public's imagination, but he also made it easier for other Latino entertainers to display their talents to English-speaking audiences in the United States. Latino musicians had been performing for Spanish-speaking audiences for decades, but language and cultural differences had kept their existence a secret to the majority of people in the United States. Martin helped change that. His success seemed to whet everyone's appetite for Latin music.

"It's been building, but this time it's a wave and it's got a lot of momentum," said Sony Music Entertainment chairman Thomas Mottola, explaining the Latin music craze that has hit the United States. "This craze, this phenomenon is not exactly new to us; it's just that everybody's catching on to it, recognizing it and jumping on the bandwagon."

GLOSSARY OF LATIN MUSICAL STYLES

Mariachi: Traditional Mexican music, often performed on streets and in restaurants. Groups of performers usually dress in traditional cowboy outfits, complete with giant sombreros. They sing and play violins, guitars, and trumpets. The songs are mainly ballads (called *corridos*) about love, death, honor, and valor. Often, all four themes can be found in the same song.

Salsa: A fast-paced Latin style, similar to disco, with African, Cuban, and Puerto Rican roots. The name *salsa* refers to the hot and spicy nature of the music, which began in New York in the 1960s and 1970s. It features an incessant beat. Several countries in Latin America have local variations on salsa, which go by such names as *merengue, tropical,* and *cumbia.*

Tejano: A musical style that emerged on the U.S. side of the Mexico-Texas border (Tejano is Spanish for "Texan") in the early twentieth century. The style developed when northern Mexican music merged with the fast-paced polka and waltz music of German immigrants in Texas. Tejano often features accordians and an oompah-pah sound.

The Pop en Español (Spanish pop) movement re-sembles "the British invasion," which brought The Beatles, the Rolling Stones, and other British musi-cians to the United States in the 1960s. What sets the Latino invasion apart, however, is the fact that it's mainly an *internal* invasion. Although some may sing in a foreign language (Spanish), the Latino artists who created the big splash in 1999 were all born or raised in the United States. Ricky Martin, for exam-ple, was born and raised in Puerto Rico, an island ter-ritory of the United States.

The new Latino artists don't play it safe. Instead of aiming to please their traditional Puerto Rican, Mexi-can, or Cuban audiences, these entertainers take aim at the hearts—and wallets—of the American main-stream. These new artists have made it cool to be Latino. Instead of trying to sound like every other English-speaking act, they celebrate their roots. They use Latino rhythms and styles that are unfamiliar to the vast majority of new fans. The artists also main-tain enough ethnic flavor to satisfy longtime fans who have followed them into the mainstream.

"I think what happened with [rhythm and blues] at Motown is what's happening with Latin music now," said record producer Emilio Estefan, recalling the 1960s. During this era, the Motown record label helped send African American performers to the top of mainstream charts. "It's like a sleeping giant wak-ing up all over the world."

In December 1999, Enrique Iglesias wowed a crowd at a holiday concert in New York City.

The first performer to successfully follow Ricky Martin across the cultural divide was Jennifer Lopez. An accomplished actor and considered one of the most beautiful women in the world, Lopez branched out into music by releasing an album in the summer of 1999. The album was a huge success, producing a number-one song and establishing Lopez as a multidimensional star.

Heartthrob Enrique Iglesias, the son of Spanish crooner Julio Iglesias, followed up the Martin and Lopez successes by producing his own number-one song, "Bailamos" (Let's Dance), and selling out arenas all over the country. He was followed in the fall of 1999 by the multitalented Marc Anthony, whose voice has been compared to that of Frank Sinatra. Anthony not only launched his own English-language album but also starred in one of the year's most anticipated movies, Martin Scorsese's *Bringing Out the Dead.*

As the Latino movement became more widespread, many people started to wonder what had triggered it. Many Latino performers had sung in English over the years, among them Ritchie Valens, Carlos Santana, Los Lobos, and Gloria Estefan, but none of them had created such a sensation. Then, in 1995, a twenty-three-year-old singer known simply as Selena was shot to death by an obsessed fan. As Lydia Martin of Knight Ridder newspapers wrote, "It was Selena's death that forced America to wake up to the Hispanic community surging around it. Her posthumously released CD, *Dreaming of You,* debuted at the top of the Billboard charts and went triple platinum. Her legacy begat Ricky Martin, [who] sparked an obsession with all things Hispanic."

Early in her career, Selena touched the lives of many Latin and Tejano music fans. But her popularity soon spread among mainstream American listeners.

Chapter **ONE**

SELENA

IN EARLY **1995,** JUST A FEW MONTHS SHORT OF
her twenty-fourth birthday, Selena Quintanilla-Perez
faced the most important moment of her young professional life. Already famous with Spanish-speaking
audiences in the United States and Latin America, Selena dreamed of bigger worlds to conquer. As she pre-
pared for a sold-out February concert at the
cavernous Houston Astrodome, she dreamed of being
world famous, like Madonna, Whitney Houston, and
Janet Jackson.

To reach the heights of those superstars, Selena real-
ized, she would have to risk alienating her most loyal
fans by singing more and more songs in English. In
fact, by the time the Astrodome concert rolled around,

13

she had already begun work on an English-language album, which she hoped would help establish her in the American pop music market.

So it was understandable that Selena was a little nervous when she decided to include a series of disco songs, sung in English, in the Astrodome show. She needn't have worried, though. Fans went wild from the moment she was introduced, and they continued to scream their approval as she performed such songs as "Last Dance," "On the Radio," and "Funky Town."

Thrown in among the medley was an old Gloria Gaynor song, "I Will Survive." Little did Selena or the sixty thousand fans at the Astrodome that day know how much that title would foretell the fate of Selena's music. The Houston show would be Selena's last. In less than three months, Selena would be killed by a crazed fan—but her music would live on.

In fact, Selena's music not only survived after her death, but her popularity actually increased to the levels she'd always wanted. Like movie stars James Dean and Marilyn Monroe, after her death Selena became bigger than life. The twenty-three-year-old woman became so famous, in fact, that many people have credited her with launching the Latin music revolution.

"The Latin explosion . . . I don't think it would be this intense or popular if Selena hadn't come along," says her husband, Chris Perez. "Really, I think she's the one who kicked the door open."

Selena would never know just how big a success she was to become.

That revolution was far in the future when Selena Quintanilla was born on April 16, 1971, in Brazosport, Texas. The third child of Abraham and Marcela Quintanilla, she grew up about sixty miles south of Houston in Lake Jackson, Texas, where her father worked as a shipping clerk at the Dow Chemical Company. Selena's father had spent years trying to succeed as a musician, singing with a band called Los Dinos. By the time Selena was born, Abraham had given up performing to work at Dow and provide for his family.

When Selena was six, she watched as her father showed her brother, A. B., how to play the guitar. All of a sudden, Abraham recalls, Selena started singing along in a voice that seemed much bigger than her body. Just as quickly, Selena's father started to devise a plan.

"I always wanted to go back into the music business, but I felt I was getting way too old and my kids were growing up," he said. "When I found out Selena could sing, that's when the wheels started turning in my mind. I saw the chance to get back in the music world through my kids. . . . I felt that Selena had it [talent] since she was a little girl. She had that extra thing that makes an artist."

Abraham set about turning his kids into musicians. He converted the family garage into a music studio. He gave A. B. a bass guitar and Selena's sister, Suzette, a set of drums. Selena, of course, was the lead singer. The trio started practicing every day after school.

In 1979 Selena's father left Dow Chemical and opened Papagayo, a Mexican restaurant in Lake Jackson. The restaurant included a stage and a dance floor. On weekends, Selena and her siblings would perform popular songs in English and a few in Spanish. Selena didn't speak much Spanish, though. Her father taught her the Spanish lyrics she needed to know to perform. Whether the song was in English or Spanish, Selena didn't need much encouragement to sing. And it didn't take long for people in town to notice her talent.

The band, called Selena y los Dinos (Selena and the Boys) in honor of Abraham's old group, soon added a lead guitarist and a keyboardist. With Selena's mother and father driving, the group began traveling all over Texas to play at weddings, small clubs, and birthday parties. Abraham was the band's manager and sound engineer, while Selena's mother, Marcela, served as the lighting technician. When the local oil business dried up in the early 1980s, many people moved away from the area, and the family restaurant failed. Selena and the band then became the sole means of support for the Quintanilla family. Selena was twelve at the time.

Although some people in town wondered if Abraham was pushing the kids too hard to succeed, others knew that the children, especially Selena, were happy. "She loved what she was doing," said Rena Dearman, the band's keyboard player when the group started touring. "She was having fun. . . . When she was on stage, she was into doing her thing."

The band's success led to its first album, *Mis Primeras Grabaciones* (My First Recordings), released

in 1984 when Selena was just thirteen. The album was
a collection of Spanish songs sung Tejano style—a traditional Mexican-border style featuring an oompah
rhythm. The album did not sell well because Los
Dinos needed more experience and better material. So
A. B. began writing new songs for the group.

Selena also needed to improve and learn more about
what it took to be a great singer. And the only way to
do that was through more performing. As the band's
schedule grew more hectic, Selena found it increas-
ingly difficult to attend school full-time. So she
dropped out and studied on her own. She eventually
earned her GED (the equivalent of a high school
diploma) when she was seventeen.

Los Dinos' true success began in 1986 with a minor
hit, "Dame un Beso" (Give Me a Kiss), from an album
called *Alpha*. The group built on that small success
with its next album, *Muñequito de Trapo* (Rag Doll),
which spawned another minor hit, "A Million to One."
The song got a lot of airplay on radio stations all over
San Antonio, a hub for Latin music. The two songs
provided Los Dinos with a growing base of Spanish-
speaking fans.

In the winter of 1986, the group's popularity was
confirmed at the Tejano Music Awards in San Antonio, where Selena was named Female Vocalist of the
Year (an honor she would receive seven years in a
row). The cover of her next album, *And the Winner Is*
(1987), featured a picture of the vivacious sixteen-

year-old proudly holding her award.

Several songs from the album received airplay, but the most memorable was the Latin classic "La Bamba." To everyone's surprise, "La Bamba" made it onto the Billboard pop music charts in August 1987, giving Selena the first national exposure of her career. To top off a great year, Selena won the coveted Entertainer of the Year award at the 1987 Tejano Music Awards. Los Dinos was also nominated for several major awards, including Single of the Year, Song of the Year, and Most Promising Band.

At about this time, José Behar, head of the newly created Capitol/EMI Latin record label, was looking for Spanish acts that could "cross over"—appeal to mainstream, English-speaking audiences. At the Tejano Music Awards in 1989, Behar approached Selena, asking if she would sign with EMI. At first Selena didn't believe Behar was serious, but he finally convinced her to sign a long-term contract. "The real reason I signed Selena . . . was not to sell a lot of records in the Latin Tejano market," Behar explains. "The reason I signed her is because I thought [she would be] the next Gloria Estefan."

The signing had the full support of Abraham Quintanilla, who saw the partnership as the boost Selena needed to make her dreams come true. "José Behar and I both shared the same vision for Selena. Putting her recording career in his able hands proved to be one of the best decisions I ever made," said Abraham.

Yolanda Saldívar headed up Selena's fan club.

After she signed with a major label, Selena's popularity skyrocketed almost immediately. Spurred on by "Buenos Amigos" (Good Friends), which hit number one on the Billboard Latin charts in 1991, Selena became a household name among Latinos in the United States. A growing legion of fans flocked to her concerts. One devoted follower, San Antonio nurse Yolanda Saldívar, established a Selena fan club.

The hits continued with "La Caracha" and "Como la Flor" (Like the Flower), which eventually became Selena's signature song. She also began making music videos, which helped introduce her to fans throughout Latin America, especially in Mexico, where Tejano music is very popular. It wasn't long before Selena was being called "the Madonna of Latin America."

It was easy to see why. As Selena's voice continued to develop, she also matured into a beautiful young woman. In 1992 she married Chris Perez, a member of her band. As a Jehovah's Witness, a member of a strict Christian group, Selena was devoutly religious. She did not drink or swear. But her onstage persona was far different from that of a happily married, religious woman. Instead of wearing the traditional country-and-western outfits favored by other female Tejano singers, Selena wore tight-fitting sequined outfits that complimented her ample curves. She usually took the stage wearing her signature bustier—a sexy, strapless top that Madonna had made trendy in the 1980s.

Romance bloomed between band members Selena and Chris Perez.

In 1993 Selena, left, accepted the award for Best Album of the Year at the 13th Annual Tejano Music Awards.

Despite her fame and growing financial success, Selena wanted much more. She had always dreamed of being famous—but famous all over the world, not just in Texas and Latin America. Selena had been born in the United States. Her primary language was English, and she wanted to conquer the English-speaking world.

To do so, she knew she would have to push beyond the boundaries of traditional Tejano music. With the help of her brother, she began incorporating elements of hip-hop, reggae, funk, salsa, and techno music into her repertoire. No song better reflected this change than "Techno Cumbia." By its very title (cumbia is a Latin American dance style), the song signaled a new style of Tejano music. The song appeared on the landmark 1994 album *Amor Prohibido* (Prohibited Love), which Selena's father considered Los Dinos' crowning achievement. The album would produce four number-one songs and became the group's biggest seller.

"By this time Selena was as happy as she'd ever been," said Abraham Quintanilla. "She was married, she had her family around her, she had become Tejano's biggest single sensation, and she had conquered all of Latin America. Indeed, Selena's music was known far and wide. Selena y los Dinos had almost single-handedly put Tejano music on the world's stage. Clearly, we had come a long way from those makeshift practice sessions in our garage in Lake Jackson."

For many years, José Behar had been trying to convince EMI's pop music division to let Selena cross over and record for a general audience. Selena's new music proved so intriguing that the pop division finally agreed to take a chance on her. By 1994 she was planning an English-language album that both she and EMI hoped would make her as big a star as Madonna or Whitney Houston.

But *Amor Prohibido* was so popular that Selena didn't have time for recording. She was in constant demand to perform in concerts, commercials, and even movies. She made her film debut as a mariachi singer in *Don*

Juan DeMarco (1995), which starred Marlon Brando and Johnny Depp. Work on her crossover album was delayed even more while she opened a line of boutiques, called Selena Etc., which helped to make her one of the richest Latin performers in the world. Her annual income was estimated by *Hispanic Business* magazine to be five million dollars.

"This is the first time I have ever made a debut album by an artist who was too busy to record for me," said Nancy Brennan, an EMI vice president, in March 1995. "How can you tell someone, 'No, I don't want you to play the Astrodome for 60,000 [fans], I want you to work on your record'? Everybody wants her."

Brennan, however, was willing to wait, because the label was confident it had a budding superstar on its hands. "I think Selena can do anything she wants to do," she said. "She can have a successful career in two languages. She's got the pipes. She's got the heart. She's got the look."

Brennan was right. But like all musicians, Selena still faced day-to-day business struggles. One problem involved Yolanda Saldívar, the head of Selena's fan club. Saldívar seemed to be wildly devoted to Selena. In addition to running the club, she even turned her home into a Selena museum. She attended all of Selena's concerts, where she screamed as if she were a lovesick teenager. Selena trusted Saldívar at first and let her manage Selena Etc.

boutiques in San Antonio and Corpus Christi.

But conflicts soon developed. In March 1995, Selena's father found several checks that Saldívar had written to herself from the fan-club bank account. He questioned whether Saldívar was stealing money from the club. But Selena refused to believe the worst about Saldívar, thinking that there had to be a good explanation for the missing money. What Selena did not know was that, about ten years before, Saldívar had been accused of stealing about nine thousand dollars when she worked as a bookkeeper for a doctor.

Eventually, even Selena grew to suspect Saldívar, and she finally decided to fire her. On March 31, 1995, Selena kissed her husband good-bye at about 9:30 A.M. She went to meet Saldívar in a room at the Days Inn, a Corpus Christi motel where she planned to give Saldívar the news. Within two hours, family members grew nervous when they did not hear from Selena as expected later that morning. By 1:00 P.M., Selena's father had received a call from the hospital. He was told that Selena had been injured. It wasn't until the family reached the hospital that they learned that Saldívar had shot Selena in the back. Selena had staggered to the motel lobby for help. She later died at the hospital.

Meanwhile, back at the Days Inn, Saldívar had jumped into a parked truck. Still armed with a gun, she held police at bay for nine hours before they talked her into surrendering. She was arrested. And by the end of 1995, Saldívar was convicted of first-degree murder and sentenced to life in prison.

The news that Selena had been shot spread quickly. Soon, hundreds of fans had gathered at the Days Inn, even before Saldívar had surrendered. In the days following the shooting, thousands of fans flocked to the motel, Selena's house, her grave, and the family recording studio. They left flowers, cards, and other articles, turning these places into memorials for the slain singer. They held prayer vigils for Selena, named their babies for her, and even erected life-size statues of her around Texas.

In a dramatic showdown, police approach the pickup truck of murder suspect Yolanda Saldívar.

Fans express their sadness and appreciation for Selena at the motel room where she was shot.

"Like grief-stricken pilgrims, Selena's fans streamed to [Corpus Christi] on the Gulf of Mexico from as far south as Colombia and as far north as Canada," the *Arizona Republic* wrote a year later. "They haven't stopped. To young Hispanics, Selena was more than a successful singer. She represented cultural pride and unity. She was their role model. She was beautiful, vibrant, proud and charming."

While Selena's family was comforted by the out-pouring of love and support, they were understand-ably shocked at how quickly Selena had been taken from them. "Selena's senseless and tragic murder plunged my family into a period of deep sadness and despair . . . a feeling of profound sorrow that to this day we have not overcome," wrote Abraham Quintanilla several years later. "Eventually, in the months following that dark day in Corpus Christi, Marcela, A. B., Suzette, and Chris agreed with me that Selena would have wanted us to go on . . . to pursue our goals and in the end, realize her dream of being successful in the mainstream pop market."

Because of Selena's dream of being a mainstream success, the family released more of her songs in a variety of posthumous albums. One of them, *Dreaming of You*, debuted at the top of the Billboard charts and sold more than three million copies.

Selena's family, from left to right, *Marcela, Suzette, Abraham, and Chris Perez*

Selena's fans, young and old, cherish the memories they have of the young singer.

Abraham Quintanilla believes that strangers were able to connect with his daughter because "she was an American girl of Mexican descent pursuing the American dream." He also believes that Selena, who was incredibly humble about her success, would have been surprised and even a little embarrassed by all the fuss that was made after her death.

And imagine Selena's reaction when Hollywood came calling. Indeed, the fervor with which Selena's fans held onto her memory caught the attention of movie producers. In 1997 a casting call went out for an actress to play the lead role in *Selena*. Eventually, Jennifer Lopez was selected for the part. Lopez bore a slight resemblance to Selena, which helped her win the role. She was also able to capture the singer's engaging personality. The movie was a huge hit. Not only was it received warmly by Selena's loyal fans, but it also fulfilled Selena's dream—making her a favorite among non-Latinos.

CHRIS PEREZ

Chris Perez was a struggling seventeen-year-old guitarist when Selena's father invited him to join Selena y los Dinos in 1988. At the time, the group was just breaking into the music business. After playing with the band for a couple of years, Perez left to pursue his own career. He came back to Los Dinos a year later, and the friendship he'd developed with Selena blossomed into love. The two were married on April 2, 1992. They spent their honeymoon touring with the band.

Since Selena's death in 1995, Perez has spent a lot of time grieving. He has also worked hard to resurrect his career, which he has directed away from Tejano music and into Rock en Español, a growing movement of Hispanic rock-and-roll musicians. He started a band called the Chris Perez Band, which includes former Los Dinos band member Joe Ojeda.

Part of the problem is that millions of Selena fans still think of Chris as "Mr. Selena"—not as an accomplished musician in his own right. "I'm really excited that people are going to be able to find out who we really are," Perez said shortly after the release of his first post-Selena album. Appropriately titled *Resurrection*, the album includes some rock songs in English. "I think with the media, a lot of the hype surrounding the movie *[Selena]* and those unauthorized books and whatever else, the focus of who I really am as a person got shifted. They relate to the person in the movie, they relate to the person in books. Sometimes I feel it's been forgotten that, first and foremost, I'm a musician." Listeners maybe catching on. *Resurrection* won a Grammy for Best Latin Rock/Alternative Performance in 2000.

According to friends, Selena would have been happy for Chris and his new career. "She always supported him 100 percent," said keyboardist Joe Ojeda. "She knew that was what he always wanted to do."

"I am not of Hispanic heritage and I must confess that until Selena's untimely death, I knew very little about Tejano music," wrote one unidentified fan on the *Latinolink* Internet site. "But I will admit that one thing her fans were right about, she was an amazing young woman. She had the voice of an angel and the charm to bring peace to the world. . . . I honestly think that Selena's memory will go on in the hearts of all her fans forever."

Singer and actor Jennifer Lopez wore one of Selena's signature gowns for a scene in the movie Selena.

Ricky Martin shows off some moves as he sings his hit single "Livin' la Vida Loca."

Chapter **TWO**

RICKY MARTIN

THE SCREAMING CAN BE HEARD EVEN BEFORE
Ricky Martin comes into view. The crowd, usually
made up of thousands of teenage girls, normally waits
for hours to see him. In some cases, fans have been
known to camp out overnight wherever Martin is appearing so they can be among the first to get a
glimpse of their hero. The roar of the crowd never
really goes away, but every once in a while, a stray
sentence or two can be made out above the screaming.

"Ricky! Te amo!" some yell in Spanish. "Ricky! I love
you!" others yell in English. "Ricky! Marry me!"
scream still others. As soon as Martin does appear, the
noise becomes deafening. It is not unusual for some
of the young girls to faint. The energy doesn't subside

33

until Martin has stopped moving his lips, shaking his hips, and waving good-bye.

From Mexico to Japan, from Canada to Australia, from India to Turkey, this scene is repeated day after day, week after week, in whatever record store, concert hall, television studio, shopping mall, or theater the young Puerto Rican heartthrob happens to be appearing that day. And these days, it seems, Ricky Martin is everywhere.

Martin is getting the kind of adoration that, in the past, has been heaped on such performers as Michael Jackson, Elvis Presley, and The Beatles. "[Ricky]

Some fans just can't get enough of Ricky!

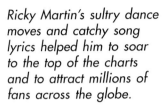

Ricky Martin's sultry dance moves and catchy song lyrics helped him to soar to the top of the charts and to attract millions of fans across the globe.

embodies our times," says his producer, Desmond Child. "He has all of the zest for life and the hope that the new millennium has in store for us."

His popularity, already huge in Spanish-speaking countries, skyrocketed in the United States in 1999 following the success of his number-one hit "Livin' la Vida Loca." Almost overnight, Martin became one of the most famous singers in the world. Soon, fans and music critics were calling him the leader of the Latin musical wave.

By his own admission, Martin does not have the most powerful singing voice. What he does have is an engaging personality, incredible good looks, and a winning stage presence. His pop and love songs are marked by a heavy beat and catchy rhythms. His energetic dancing and good-natured flirting have an intoxicating effect on female fans.

Performing comes naturally to Martin, who has spent most of his life onstage or on television. He was born Enrique Martin Morales IV near San Juan, Puerto Rico, on December 24, 1971. Although his parents divorced when he was two, they provided a comfortable life for their son. They shared custody, with Ricky moving back and forth between each parent's home whenever he wanted.

His father, Enrique Martin Negroni, was a psychologist, and his mother, Nereida Morales, was an accountant. Neither of his parents had a performing background, but that did not stop the youngster, whom they nicknamed Kiki and later Ricky, from choosing to enter show business. In fact, the singer recalls walking up to his father at age six and informing him of this decision.

"The first thing [my father] said was 'It looks great, fame, travel, girls, concerts. But there's a lot more than that,'" Martin recalled. "Behind the scenes it's a lot of work, you have to be very disciplined."

Almost immediately, Ricky's parents made an effort to help their son become an entertainer. They encouraged him to appear in school plays and sing in church choirs. They enrolled him in singing lessons. His mother began taking Ricky to concerts by legendary Latin American performers such as Tito Puente and Celia Cruz. These shows only fueled Ricky's desire to be onstage himself. Finally, his parents began taking him to audition for parts in television commercials, some of

A young Tito Puente plays timbales (kettle drums). His energetic performances and great musical talent made Puente popular with audiences until his death in June 2000.

which he was lucky enough to land. So at the age of six, Ricky Martin became a professional performer.

By 1984 twelve-year-old Ricky had already appeared in more than fifty commercials. But more than anything, he wanted to perform onstage. Specifically, he wanted to join Menudo, a singing group made up of teenage Puerto Rican boys that was a worldwide hit among teenage girls. The boys sang in both English and Spanish. Martin had auditioned twice for the

In his first big break, Ricky, second from left, *joined Menudo, the popular boy band from Puerto Rico.*

group, at ages eight and eleven, but was turned down because he was too young. Finally, when he auditioned again at age twelve, the group's managers were convinced that they might have a star on their hands.

Martin can still recall the excitement he felt at being asked to join the exclusive group after his third audition. He told his parents that he was going to become famous. "I didn't want to be a singer, not then," Martin said. "What I wanted was to be in Menudo. I wanted to give concerts, to travel, to meet the pretty girls."

Life with Menudo provided Martin with all of those opportunities, but the job was more difficult than it appeared. The group traveled with tutors. The young singers had to make time for schoolwork while performing hundreds of shows each year. Menudo was such a moneymaker that managers left nothing to chance. The boys were coached not only on how to perform but also on how to dress, act, and speak in public.

The pressure was intense. Many of the boys burned out and left Menudo not long after joining. Others misbehaved, and management asked them to leave. But Ricky thrived with the group. "Ricky had that special personality. He could handle himself," said Edgardo Diaz, the group's manager.

Martin's parents, however, did not handle their son's success as easily as he did. They started arguing with each other about Ricky's career. At one point, Ricky's father asked him to choose between the two parents. This request upset Ricky, who chose to stay with his mother. He became so angry that he even stopped talking to his father for about ten years.

Menudo taught Ricky a lot about singing and performing. It also taught him about discipline and hard work. After reaching Menudo's mandatory retirement age of seventeen, Ricky left the group to finish high school in San Juan. Then he set out to conquer the world of show business.

After he graduated in 1989, Ricky moved to New York City for a few months. Then he set off for Mexico City, where he worked at both singing and acting. He landed a job on a Spanish-language soap opera, which eventually led to starring roles in Mexican movies. He also appeared in a long-running Mexico City musical called *Mama Ama el Rock* (Mama Loves Rock).

He recorded several albums. His first one, titled *Ricky Martin*, reached gold-record status (500,000 copies sold) in Mexico, Chile, Argentina, Puerto Rico, and the United States. His second album, *Me Amarás* (You Will Love Me), proved equally successful. Martin set forth to conquer the English-speaking United States.

He moved to Los Angeles and won a job on the popular daytime soap opera *General Hospital*. In his role as Miguel Morez, a bartender who moonlights as a singer, Martin was a huge success. He eventually parlayed that part into a starring role as Marius in the Broadway production of *Les Misérables*. His third album, *A Medio Vivir* (Living Halfway), was released in 1997. Within six months of the release, it had sold more than 500,000 copies.

Although Martin wouldn't become a household name in the United States until 1999, many argue that his rise to superstar status began a year earlier with the release of his fourth album, *Vuelve* (Return). It went gold and eventually sold more than six million copies.

In July 1998, Martin was asked to perform at the finals of the World Cup soccer tournament in France.

Exploring his acting ability, Ricky made his way to the daytime soap opera General Hospital. *Here he poses with costar Lily Melgar.*

For Martin, a lifelong soccer fan, this invitation was a dream come true. He sang a song called "La Copa de la Vida" (later released in English as "The Cup of Life") before one of the largest television audiences in history—more than two billion people.

Vuelve earned Martin a nomination for the music industry's most prestigious award, the Grammy, in the Best Latin Album category. And partly because of the success of his World Cup performance, he was invited to sing "The Cup of Life" in February 1999 at the Grammy Awards ceremony in New York City.

Martin recalls, "I was anxious about it but said, 'Hey you've been doing this since [you were] 12 years old so go out and have fun.' I was trying to go out there and have fun, trying not to think about the fact that Céline Dion, Madonna, Pavarotti and Sting, the 'industry,' was there. They've seen it all and they've heard it all."

But Martin gave a sizzling performance that brought the jaded audience of industry bigwigs to its feet. While dozens of performers took the stage that night, he was the only one to receive a standing ovation. He also won his first Grammy.

Ricky Martin showed off his Grammy Award in 1999.

As the acclaim mounted, it was no surprise that people went crazy when Martin's first English-language album (also called *Ricky Martin*) was released in May 1999. Within days, it was the best-selling album in the country. The first single, "Livin' la Vida Loca," immediately shot to number one, and the song's video became an instant staple on cable television.

The album also featured Martin singing a duet, "Be Careful" (Cuidado con Mi Corazón), with Madonna. Martin had met the pop diva in Austria in the early 1990s. She had cemented the relationship by kissing him after his spectacular performance at the Grammy Awards. She was so impressed by Martin's music that she asked to sing with him, a request that eventually led to "Be Careful." "I'm not sure why she chose me," Martin said about the duet. "But when Madonna asks you to do something you don't really think twice. She is a legend."

With the album's success, Martin found that his life was no longer his own. He could not go out in public without causing a stir or a traffic jam. Dozens of Ricky Martin websites sprang up on the Internet. On these sites, fans debated not only the merits of his music but also which woman he should marry. The night before a three-song miniconcert on NBC's early morning *Today* show, hundreds of fans camped out on the streets surrounding the television station. The crowd eventually grew to more than five thousand, which surprised not only the show's producers but

In New York City, Ricky's fans came out to see him perform for the Today show.

also the New York Police Department. Officers had to close blocks and blocks of streets to car traffic around the station.

All of a sudden, Latin music was white hot. Latin rhythms "always have been part of popular music," said Thomas Mottola, chairman of Sony Music Entertainment. "But without question, Ricky was the fuse that lit the dynamite, and that Grammy performance sort of set the world on fire."

As the leader of the Latin invasion, Ricky Martin takes his role seriously. He turned down a chance to star with Jennifer Lopez in a remake of the movie *West Side Story* because he thought that the film would promote negative stereotypes about Puerto Ricans. The movie, based on a musical from the 1950s, is a love story about a young couple caught in a war between rival white and Puerto Rican gangs.

By all accounts, Ricky Martin is handling his success remarkably well. Most everyone who knows him mentions his polite manners and quick mind. He is modest when talking about his fame. And although he took the United States by storm—seemingly overnight—he is quick to point out that the success actually involved years of hard work. "Instead of grabbing America by storm, America caught me," Martin explains. "Ever since [the Grammys] I've been living, literally a vida loca—the crazy life."

He is very much aware of the pitfalls that await celebrities, especially those who become so popular that they lose all sense of privacy. "I pray for control of my emotions," Martin says. "All this glamour, adrenaline and euphoria that fame presents can seduce and destroy you if you're not in touch with your feelings. I don't want to sound dramatic, but it can kill you." One of the ways in which Martin stays focused is by eating breakfast each day by himself. No managers. No secretaries. No phone calls. No work. Just Martin, his yogurt, his cereal, his juice, and his pancakes or French toast.

Even with all his success and promise of future conquests, Martin admits that everything is not perfect in his world. One thing still bothers him: "I have no butt," he laments. "Everybody tells me that. It's tiny. Yes it is. What can I do? Not even rock climbing helps."

Oh well, you can't have everything.

Hats off to Jennifer Lopez!

Chapter **THREE**

JENNIFER LOPEZ

WHEN JENNIFER LOPEZ DECIDED TO RELEASE AN album of songs during the summer of 1999, many people in the entertainment industry were surprised. They couldn't understand why Lopez, an accomplished actor, would risk venturing into the music business. If the album was a flop, not only would it embarrass Lopez but it might even damage her career. Critics assumed that Lopez, a New Yorker of Puerto Rican descent, was just trying to capitalize on the success of Ricky Martin and the growing taste for Latino music in the United States.

Imagine the critics' surprise when the album, a collection of English and Spanish ballads that Lopez described as "Latin soul," shot to the top of the charts. Propelled by a song that quickly went to number one, the album made the popular actor even more popular. Suddenly, the music industry and the public were intrigued by this woman who seemed to have so many different talents.

The curiosity surrounding Lopez only grew as people tried to decipher the meaning of the album's title. She called the work *On the 6*, and fans immediately wondered why. Reporters asked her about the title constantly. The answer proved somewhat surprising.

Jennifer Lopez has a reputation for being outspoken and sometimes even outrageous. She also has a healthy ego. So industry experts and music critics expected Lopez to give her debut album an outrageous title or to name it after herself. Instead, the native New Yorker surprised people by going the sentimental route. It turns out that when Lopez was first starting out in show business, she would often get up early to catch the subway into Manhattan from her home in the Castle Hill section of the Bronx.

"I used to take the No. 6 train downtown from the Bronx," said Lopez. Like hundreds of other aspiring performers, she spent hours every day practicing and auditioning in Manhattan. "I was about 18. [The title] was about making the transition from this girl in Castle Hill who could have been a lawyer to dancing, singing and auditioning, letting the artist in me come on."

Those closest to Lopez, however, were not surprised by her sentimentality. In fact, family and friends prob-

Jennifer sang to a crowd of soccer fans before a 1999 World Cup match between the United States and China.

ably would have been surprised if this self-proclaimed "homegirl from the 'hood" had not included her old neighborhood in one of the most important works of her professional life.

Maintaining ties to the Bronx and the working-class neighborhood of Castle Hill has always been important to Lopez. That's where she was born on July 24,

1970, the second of three girls. That's where she got her first taste of performing onstage. That's where she developed her dreams and made lifelong friends. In fact, her personal assistant has been her best friend since kindergarten.

"I am still the same girl who grew up in the Bronx . . . with my head full of limitless dreams," says Lopez. "I still wake up thinking about everything that I want to achieve . . . feeling that I can't stop . . . that I have to win an Oscar . . . make better movies . . . sing in big arenas . . . I feel like I can do anything, any kind of role. I am not afraid of anybody."

Lopez credits her fearlessness in large part to growing up in the Bronx, which has a well-deserved reputation as one of the toughest areas of New York. Lopez says that the environment taught her to be tough and how to handle rejection. It taught her to stay focused. It showed her the benefits of hard work. It also helped her remain down-to-earth, according to her family.

"I am very proud of my daughter," says Jennifer's mom, Guadalupe Lopez, a kindergarten teacher at Holy Family School in the Bronx. "She lives in North Hollywood in an enormous apartment that has four bedrooms, but her heart will always be here in the Bronx. . . . I know she will never go Hollywood. That's not who she is."

While Lopez may never "go Hollywood"—flaunt her celebrity status and put on airs—she has known since she was young that she wanted to be a star. She was bitten by the show-business bug after watching movies starring Ava Gardner, Rita Hayworth, and Marilyn Monroe. Jennifer took as her role model another multitalented Puerto Rican woman, Rita Moreno, one of the few entertainers in the world to win all three major performing arts awards—the Oscar, the Tony, and the Emmy. Perhaps that explains why Lopez's favorite movie is *West Side Story*, the film for which Rita Moreno earned her Oscar.

Rita Moreno, center, *kicks up her heels in a scene from the movie* West Side Story.

As a teenager in Castle Hill, Jennifer performed gymnastics, played softball, and competed nationally in track. She worked out nearly every day. But she participated in athletics mainly as a way to stay in shape. She wanted to be a dancer or a movie star, and she knew that her physique would be important to her success.

Jennifer got her first stage experience singing and dancing in musical theater, landing jobs as a teenager in a European tour of *Golden Musicals of Broadway* and a Japanese tour of *Synchronicity*. Apart from giving her some much needed experience, the jobs made her more determined than ever to move beyond the confines of her working-class neighborhood.

Jennifer Lopez's high school yearbook photo

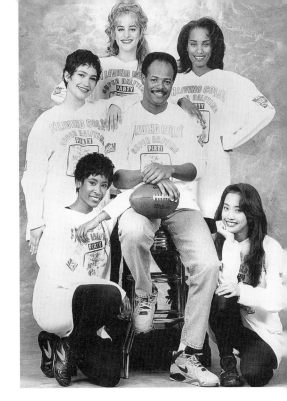

Lopez, standing on left, made her television debut as a *Fly Girl* in the 1990s hit TV show In Living Color.

Another break came in 1990, when Jennifer beat out thousands of other dancers nationwide to become one of the Fly Girls, a group of dancers who performed on the Fox television comedy *In Living Color.* As part of the job, Jennifer had to move to Los Angeles—away from her beloved New York. In Los Angeles, Lopez parlayed her Fly Girl role into a part as a dancer in a Janet Jackson video. Within a few months, Lopez was also able to land some acting roles—minor parts in several short-lived television programs.

Just as Lopez appeared to be on her way to an act-ing career, she was faced with having to make a tough decision. Janet Jackson's managers offered Jennifer a full-time job dancing on the next Janet Jackson world tour. The job meant a year and a half of steady work—a godsend to any struggling performer. But ever a risk taker, Lopez decided to take a chance on her future as an actress. She turned down the dancing job, choosing instead to pursue a role in the television series *South Central.*

Even though the series did not last long, joining the show proved to be the right decision for Lopez. She wanted to move beyond dancing and into movies. Her *South Central* role attracted attention, and Jennifer was able to land parts in two other television series, *Second Chances* and *Malibu Road.* Neither series lasted very long either, but they did lead Lopez to a starring role in a 1993 made-for-TV movie called *Nurses on the Line: The Crash of Flight 7.*

Her big break onto the silver screen came in 1995, when she was selected for a starring role in the movie *Mi Familia* (My Family), a story about a Mexican family over several generations. Suddenly, Jennifer Lopez was hot, and she made the most of it. Her on-screen charisma attracted the attention of some of the most famous directors and actors in Hollywood. Francis Ford Coppola saw Lopez in *Mi Familia* and hired her to play Robin Williams's teacher in *Jack.* Her next role put her opposite none other than Jack Nicholson in the movie *Blood and Wine.* She then landed a starring role as a police detective in the action movie *Money Train,* which also featured Woody Harrelson and Wesley Snipes. While the movie was not a big success, Lopez got some good reviews for her acting.

In a dramatic scene from the movie Anaconda, *Lopez's character tries to pull rapper Ice Cube from the grips of the giant snake.*

As Lopez's stature increased, so did her marketability. She soon became the highest paid Latina actress ever, earning one million dollars per film for such high-profile movies as *Anaconda,* with rapper Ice Cube, and *U Turn,* directed by Oliver Stone. Lopez was on a roll. She followed *U Turn* with her most critically acclaimed performance, starring opposite George Clooney in *Out of Sight* (1998). In this film, Lopez played a U.S. marshal, and many movie critics thought she deserved an Academy Award nomination for her work.

Lopez's signature role, and the one that made her a true megastar, was the lead in *Selena* (1997), the story of Tejano singer Selena Quintanilla-Perez. Lopez was

Lopez belts out a tune during the filming of Selena.

selected from more than twenty-two hundred actresses to play the part. The movie was a phenomenal success, grossing almost $100 million at the box office. The movie also introduced English-speaking America to Selena's music, made Jennifer Lopez a bona fide star, and awakened Corporate America to the enormous and growing presence—and buying power—of Latinos in the United States.

"She called me at one in the morning to ask me what I thought about the movie," Guadalupe Lopez said after seeing her daughter in the premiere. "I told her I loved it, and I did. I am trying to get all of my Latino friends to go to the movie . . . to show people that the Latinos have a buck. It's important to be there for . . . box office reasons."

The film, which opens with Selena giving a concert at the Houston Astrodome, also reawakened a dream in Lopez—the desire to record an album and perform her own concerts. During the filming, Lopez sang before thirty-five hundred screaming fans who were brought in for the Astrodome scene. (Later, Selena's real voice and music were dubbed into the concert scenes.) Although the fans were supposed to be cheering for Selena, they were also cheering for Lopez, who looked like Selena, danced like Selena, and even sang like Selena.

The excitement of being onstage sparked something inside Lopez. "I've almost forgotten how much I like to perform onstage because I've been caught up in doing films," she said. "It was great getting in front of an audience, getting that immediate response. . . . I liked it! And that week I told my managers I wanted to record something. I've gotta record an album. I love doing it so much."

"The idea to do an album is not a gimmick," she explained. "When I did *Selena,* it all came back again, having that interaction with the fans and public, which you don't get with movies. I missed that very much. I missed the excitement of the stage, which I had early in my career with the musical theater."

While *Selena* proved to be a major turning point in Lopez's career, the movie caused a stir for other reasons.

Unlike most female movie stars and runway models, Lopez is not painfully thin. Selena also had a curvy figure, which she did not mind showing off by wearing revealing outfits onstage. To fit her movie character, Lopez also wore revealing clothes while filming *Selena's* concert scenes. The result? Fans, especially young Latina and black women, went crazy for Lopez.

Nely Galán, the female president of the Spanish-language television network Telemundo, explains, "[Latina] girls grow up with hourglass figures and big butts, and the women you see become movie stars are tall, thin and hipless, more like Gwyneth Paltrow. Now all these Latina girls are going, 'Good, my butt is hot.'" Because she wasn't rail thin, Lopez had broken the mold and allowed millions of women to feel good about their bodies. Suddenly, it was okay for women to have hips, curves, and a big backside.

Lopez's derriere became so famous that it was even the focus of a photo spread in *Vanity Fair* magazine in 1998. She took all this attention in stride. She even called herself "the guitar girl" because, she says, her body resembles that musical instrument. She likes to point out that most Hispanic females have similar builds and should be proud of them. "Latinas and black women have a certain body type," says Lopez. "We're curvy. It's in the history books. I didn't start a revolution. But I don't mind if all the big-butted women in the world are a little happier because of a few cameramen's obsession with my behind."

Not afraid of showing off
her curves, Lopez often
wears revealing outfits.

Along with all of this positive publicity, Lopez has become something of a lightning rod because of her
strong personality, which many have labeled as "ag-
gressive" and "driven." Some people call her ambitious, as if it is a dirty word. "Why," she wonders, "is
[ambition] a bad thing with women? I mean, yeah, I'm
ambitious, but so is everybody—men, women. . . . If
going after things and accomplishing things makes you
happy, then fine. If staying home and baby-sitting
makes you happy, that's cool."

Still, Lopez admits that her drive to succeed has hurt her personally. She was married briefly in 1996 to Ojani Noa, a waiter she met in Miami while filming *Blood and Wine*. The couple married less than a year after meeting and divorced quietly a year after that. Part of the reason for the breakup, she says, was that Noa had trouble dealing with her success. He hoped she would stay home more often, but she preferred performing. Although she realizes that her hectic schedule could get in the way of true romance, she is unwilling to pass up professional opportunities that present themselves. "I would hate to be a 50-year-old and think, I should have done that back then," Lopez says.

Another trait that has gotten Lopez into trouble is her willingness to speak her mind. In a celebrated interview with *Movieline* magazine in February 1999, she spoke bluntly about other actors. She said that Gwyneth Paltrow was more famous for dating Brad Pitt than for her acting, that Cameron Diaz was just a lucky model, and that she didn't understand why everyone loved Winona Ryder. The interview angered many people in Hollywood, and Lopez learned to tone down her public comments from then on.

Lopez says that she is just a regular person. Regular in private, perhaps, but once onstage or before a camera she displays an extraordinary combination of talent that few other performers can match. She is an acclaimed actress, an accomplished dancer, and, as she proved with *On the 6*, a hit singer.

SEAN "PUFFY" COMBS

ean Combs, also known by his stage name Puff Daddy, is one of the most successful and outspoken performers and producers in all of rap music. Yet Combs was surprisingly coy and quiet in 1999 whenever the subject of Jennifer Lopez came up. Gossip columnists and music fans kept insisting that Combs and Lopez were an item—that, in fact, they were going to get married. Combs insisted that he and Jennifer were just friends, even though he was often seen with her.

The two met in the mid-1990s, and their relationship blossomed during 1998 and 1999. Finally, at the end of 1999, Combs publicly declared his love for the Puerto Rican beauty. "I never had anyone love me the way she loves me," he said. "I love her and, hopefully, one day I will be able to marry her." Shortly before Christmas, Combs placed an $85,000 engagement ring on Lopez's finger.

Combs, acknowledged as a visionary when it comes to producing hit records, worked with Lopez in creating *On the 6* and the accompanying music videos. He also advised her on her career, often attending her photo shoots and publicity tours. Together they are one of the richest couples in the entertainment industry. He makes an estimated $50 million a year as the head of Bad Boy Entertainment. She makes at least $5 million per movie, on top of royalties she will receive for her hugely successful album.

Lopez's acting talent was recognized at the 1999 American Latino Media Arts Awards. She received an award for outstanding actress in a feature film (Out of Sight) in a crossover role.

On the 6 incorporates salsa and other Latin styles with the rhythm and blues and hip-hop music Lopez heard growing up in the Bronx. Like Ricky Martin, Lopez does not have a strong singing voice. She has a sultry, throaty, and understated style. Strong voice or not, her first single, "If You Had My Love," went to number one and knocked Ricky Martin's "Livin' la

Vida Loca" from the top spot in the country. Lopez even cowrote three of the songs on the album.

She thinks a lot of young people will identify with the album because it expresses common American experiences and influences. "I think it appeals definitely to my generation of people, who . . . had Latin parents or parents of different ethnicity, who have that strong background but also grew up here in America," Lopez says. "It's like, you know all sides. That's what I felt like I needed my music to reflect."

Lopez likes to think that, beyond her impact as an entertainer, she is having a broader impact on society. She believes she is a reflection of the changing nature of the country—specifically the changing nature of Latinos in the United States. "For our parents it was more about survival and struggle and moving to a new country," she says. For her generation of Latinos, Lopez explains, it's all about possibilities.

Marc Anthony might not have Ricky Martin's dance moves, but Anthony's strong singing voice has impressed music-industry bigwigs and fans alike.

Chapter **FOUR**

MARC ANTHONY

MARC ANTHONY IS WIDELY REGARDED AS THE most talented salsa singer in the world. Billy Joel can't wait to record with him. Michael Jackson thinks he sings like an angel. And critics have compared him, because of his voice and stage presence, to "Old Blue Eyes"—Frank Sinatra.

"I was born to sing," Anthony says. "It's never been a question for me." Before moving to New York in the 1950s, Marc's father, Felipe Muniz, was a guitarist and composer in Puerto Rico. When Marc was born on September 16, 1968, Felipe named the boy Marco Antonio Muniz, after a famous Mexican ballad singer.

Although Felipe did not play music professionally in New York, he still enjoyed listening to the music of his homeland. Each weekend, Felipe and his wife, Guillermina, would invite friends to their home in the East Harlem section of the Bronx. Before the night was through, Felipe would always put his small son Marc on the kitchen table to sing for the group. One night, as Marc stood on the table and sang, his sister-in-law began to cry—the boy's beautiful voice had moved her to tears.

At age seven, Marc asked his parents to enroll him in the East Harlem School of Music. A dedicated student, he never missed a class. His interest in music, he recalls, helped him in a number of ways. First, Marc stuttered when he spoke—but not when he sang. Also, Marc's skinny physique initially made him an inviting target for neighborhood bullies. Again, music came to his rescue. "The baddest guys on the block were my friends," he explained. "They protected me. 'That kid's gonna be somebody,' they'd say. I'd sing for them, make them laugh. I was like the most protected kid on the block."

As Marc's interest in music grew, he thought about singing professionally. Everyone assumed he would sing salsa. Salsa was very popular in the 1970s, especially in Puerto Rico and in New York's Latino neighborhoods. Nowhere was the music more prevalent than in Marc's own home, where his older brothers constantly played salsa music.

But while Marc was sure he would be a singer someday, he was equally certain that he would do his singing in English, not Spanish. Despite hearing Spanish all the time, at home and on the street, Marc did not speak Spanish fluently. And he did not like Spanish music. Like many American children, Marc preferred rock and roll. He imagined himself becoming the next Barry Manilow or Billy Joel, not the next Tito Puente or Rubén Blades (both salsa singers). His opposition to singing in Spanish only intensified when his parents suggested that he sing romantic Spanish ballads called boleros. Marc simply did not think that salsa and bolero music were cool.

"My older brothers listened to salsa, and my parents used to play the old bolero music, and I shunned both," Marc said. "When your friends would be over you'd be like 'Turn that off! God, that old people music.'"

At age twelve, Marc landed his first singing job. He was hired to record voice-overs—songs to be used in television commercials. Suddenly, everything seemed possible to Marc. He told his mother that one day he was going to sell out New York's most famous arena, Madison Square Garden. "I always knew that I would accomplish anything I set my mind to," he said. "No doubt ever. . . . Anything I apply myself to I do to the best of my ability. I never doubted that my day would come. If I did I would have given up a long time ago."

At Julia Richman High School, Marc was known as the class clown, but he was completely serious about his music. He began to sing freestyle house music—

RUBÉN BLADES

R ubén Blades is a poet, an actor, a Harvard-trained lawyer, a former presidential candidate in his native Panama, and one of the world's greatest salsa singers. Yet he is probably best known in the United States as a supporting actor in several run-of-the-mill Hollywood movies.

Blades was born and raised in Panama City, Panama, in 1948. His parents were both in show business. His mother sang in cabarets, and his father played conga drums in a band, although he eventually became a police officer.

Although the boy wanted to follow in their musical footsteps, his parents insisted that he get an education first. They sent him to the University of Panama to study law, which he did while singing with local bands. When he graduated, he took a job as a lawyer for the Bank of Panama, although his interest in music remained strong.

sort of a combination of hip-hop and disco—in New York nightclubs. He wrote songs for neighborhood friends, including a singer named Sa-Fire, who was also trying to break into the music business. She

A trip to New York City in 1974 changed his life. Intrigued by the growing popularity of salsa music in the city, Blades took a job with Fania records—in the mail room. He was finally able to convince executives there that he had what it took to be a singer. In 1978 he teamed up with Willie Colón, a famous trombone player, to record *Siembra* (Planting Season) one of the best-selling salsa albums of all time.

After this success, Blades started to experiment with his music, using synthesizers instead of the traditional horns and adding a little bit of rock and roll to his brand of salsa. He also introduced poetry and serious themes into his music. He was more apt to sing about politics than partying. Salsa traditionalists were shocked. They called him a traitor and not a true salsa singer. His response? Modern times called for modern lyrics and modern methods of producing music. Like Marc Anthony, Rubén Blades took up acting after becoming famous as a singer. He has appeared in several films, including *Crossover Dreams*, *Predator II*, and *Cradle Will Rock*. He also appeared with Marc Anthony in Paul Simon's Broadway play, *The Capeman*.

In the late 1980s, at the height of his popularity, Blades took time off from music to earn his master's degree in international law from Harvard University. He then returned to Panama to found a political party called Papa Egoro, which means Mother Earth in a Panamanian dialect. In May 1994, Blades made a strong but unsuccessful run for his country's presidency. He came in third, with about 20 percent of the vote in the general election.

hired Marc to sing background vocals on her album. Eventually, one of the songs Marc wrote for Sa-Fire, "Boy I've Been Told," made it to number one on the Billboard dance charts.

After high school, Anthony started branching out from the club scene, singing background vocals for such groups as the Latin Rascals and Menudo (which at the time had just hired a singer named Ricky Martin). Anthony composed two songs and sang background for Menudo, but he never got onstage with the group. He did not fit Menudo's cute, teen-idol image— Marc jokes that he wasn't good-looking enough for the group. Instead, he sang offstage into a microphone.

Anthony finally went solo after teaming up with New York record producer and DJ "Little" Louie Vega. The two had met on the club scene. Their partnership grew when they worked together on a film called *East Side Story.* Anthony starred in the film, and Little Louie wrote the score. The movie was never released, but Little Louie was so impressed with Anthony that he helped him land a contract for his first album, *When the Night Is Over,* in 1991.

Although Anthony sang most of the songs in English, he included two Spanish songs on the album. He was accompanied on these songs by Tito Puente, a salsa music legend, and several other Latin luminaries. "Ride on the Rhythm," one of the album's songs, reached number one on the Billboard Tropical charts, proving that Anthony could appeal to a Spanish-language audience. The slide toward salsa had begun.

On November 22, 1991, Anthony joined Tito Puente onstage at Madison Square Garden to celebrate the salsa great's one hundredth album. A few months

The silver-haired Puente was always a crowd pleaser.

later, Anthony became a full-blown salsa convert. The moment came while he was driving in Manhattan with friends. The car was stopped in a traffic jam in front of Madison Square Garden when Little Louie's sister stuck a cassette in the tape deck. On came a Spanish ballad called "Hasta Que Te Conocí" (Until I Met You) sung by a Mexican singer named Juan Gabriel. The song's beauty hit Anthony like a lightning bolt. He recalls imagining what the tune would sound like as a salsa song. He knew he had to record it. He jumped out of the car, ran to a phone, and called his manager. He wanted to become a salsa singer, he said, but in his own way and his own style.

Ralph Mercado, head of the RMM record label, told Anthony that he first had to get some exposure within the salsa industry. He had to perform in concert so that fans would get to know him. Mercado arranged for Anthony to perform in Los Angeles at a Latin music convention. True to his word that he wouldn't change his style, Anthony appeared onstage looking like anyone but a salsa singer. Instead of wearing the typical salsa singer's gold chains and open-collared shirt, he dressed in jeans and a T-shirt. Anthony was nervous during the show—so nervous that he didn't even notice when the audience gave him a standing ovation.

"Marc has the charism. . . a special quality," Mercado said in describing that show. "Marc had about $10 worth of clothes on him, looking all shabby, and he had long hair in a ponytail. But when I put him on the stage the place went crazy. These are people in the business who have heard it all and are tired of it, and when they get excited, it means something. I knew right away we got something happening here. I could hear the money, you know?"

In 1992 Anthony released his first salsa record, *Otra Nota* (Another Note). He included his version of "Hasta Que Te Conocí," giving the pop ballad a disco-salsa flavor. The combination was explosive. Anthony also mixed gospel and rhythm and blues into the other salsa songs, shattering everyone's notion of what salsa should be. Although the album sold more copies than any album in salsa history, it stirred up quite a controversy, especially among older and more traditional salsa fans.

"I have a different outlook on salsa," Anthony said. "When I recorded my first album, I didn't know anything about technique. People sent me cassettes, traditionalists, and said, learn this. You're doing it all wrong. I said no way. Let me contribute something new. I just closed my eyes and did it the way I heard it, from my experience, and, thank God I did it that way, because now, looking back, I can say I have a style of music that is mine."

Part of the problem for traditional salsa fans was that Anthony, with his T-shirts and jeans, looked more like a hip-hop artist than a salsa singer. He was skinny, he wore glasses, and he couldn't dance very well. The quality of his voice, however, was enough to convince audiences that they were listening not only to something new but also something very special. The album proved especially popular with urban Latino youths, who recognized the bicultural Anthony as one of their own.

In 1994 *Otra Nota* earned Anthony numerous honors, including Billboard's Best New Artist of the Year award and the Lo Nuestro—the most prestigious salsa award, presented by the Univision television network. Building on this success, Anthony sought to push the boundaries even further on his next album. This time, instead of stirring up a little controversy, Anthony's album created a full-blown salsa revolution.

Marc Anthony signed autographs after the release of his self-titled CD, Marc Anthony.

Todo a Su Tiempo (Everything in Its Time), released in 1995, sold more than 800,000 copies and contained seven hit singles. The album garnered Anthony his first Grammy nomination and Billboard's Hot Tropical Artist of the Year award in 1995 and 1996. The album stayed at the top of Billboard's Latin charts for more than two years. But more than anything, it got the attention of music critics. One after another, they wrote that *Todo a Su Tiempo* marked a turning point in salsa music and that Anthony had revolutionized the genre.

Todo a Su Tiempo was "a set of nine swirling, complexly layered dance tunes that shimmered with '90s pop craft . . . yet resonated with Latin traditions," said a writer for the *Village Voice*. "*Todo a Su Tiempo* reinvented salsa. It became . . . one of those touchstone pop albums that reveals and opens a new set of cultural possibilities—and made a strong argument for

Puerto Rican culture as the heartbeat of contemporary
New York."

In October 1997, Anthony fulfilled his promise to his
mother when he sold out Madison Square Garden.
More than seventeen thousand fans packed the arena,
producing the largest box-office take for a salsa show
in history. Anthony's third salsa album, *Contra la
Corriente* (Against the Current), was released a month
later, and it broke all sales records for salsa music. It
went gold in both the United States and Puerto Rico
and won honors in Billboard's Latin and Tropical cat-
egories. In a hint of things to come, *Time* magazine
named *Contra la Corriente* one of the top ten albums
of the year, regardless of genre. In 1999 *Contra la Corriente* would even bring Marc Anthony a Grammy
Award.

Singing salsa music was proving to be easy for Anthony. But speaking Spanish was more difficult, especially as he became more and more popular in Latin
America. Despite hearing Spanish at home, Anthony
was not fluent in his parents' native language. The
world's most famous salsa singer had to take Spanish
lessons so that he could sing fluently in Spanish and
conduct interviews with the Spanish-language media.

"Learning the lyrics and singing them [in Spanish]
was no problem," he said. "But my God, it was the
most exhausting thing, those press conferences [in
Spanish] at seven in the morning in places like
Colombia where you couldn't even make a reference

in English ... because they wouldn't get it. But I'm a quick learner and now it's second nature."

Having conquered the salsa world, Anthony was eager to broaden his horizons and maybe even return to singing in English. His record label, RMM, did not like the idea, however. RMM head Ralph Mercado feared that his label would lose millions of dollars, and the fans' support, if Anthony were to cross *back* over to English.

The disagreement only intensified a feud that had begun the year before, when one of Anthony's checks had bounced. Anthony had asked his stepbrother, Bigram Zayas, to look into his finances. Zayas, who worked for an investment firm in Connecticut, discovered that Anthony had not been receiving the proper payments from RMM. The animosity between Mercado and Anthony grew even worse when Anthony did not show up to perform at a benefit concert that Mercado had arranged in honor of RMM's tenth anniversary. Anthony said he was never told about the concert.

Anthony decided he wanted out of his contract with RMM, and he asked Zayas to be his new manager. Zayas shared Anthony's desire to expand musically, and he was confident that Anthony could make it on his own. To prove it, Zayas suggested that Anthony give a second Madison Square Garden show—without the help of his record label. The brothers would pay all the expenses and reap all of the profits if the show were successful. The show was a sellout. Anthony and Zayas even had to sell seats behind the stage.

The hostility with the record company continued. In 1998 Anthony sued the label to break his contract, vowing never to sing for RMM again. The company sued back, claiming that Anthony had not fulfilled his commitment to record five albums. The battle seemed headed to court, but the dispute was eventually settled before trial with the help of Columbia Records, which wanted to sign Anthony. Columbia, a subsidiary of Sony Music Entertainment, bought out the rest of Anthony's contract, although Anthony gave RMM the right to issue a greatest hits album before the end of 1999.

Columbia planned on making Marc Anthony a star of the first order. In June, it gave him a $40 million contract, which allowed him to expand into the English-language, pop-ballad genre. "I've worked with incredible singers my whole career, and for me, [Anthony] stands out as one of the greatest singers in the world," said Sony's Thomas Mottola.

Mottola was not the only one who noticed Anthony's star power. Singer Paul Simon had also heard Anthony and asked him to participate in a project he was planning—a Broadway musical about Salvador Agron, a Puerto Rican gang member convicted of stabbing two people to death in 1959. Anthony was hired to play the lead role. The musical, called *The Capeman* and described as a "pop opera," also starred

Anthony received flowers and applause for his acting debut in The Capeman.

Panamanian salsa singer Rubén Blades, a close friend of Anthony's. But the show proved to be a disaster. Critics called it boring. The lone exception to the criticism? Marc Anthony, who wowed the audience with his exceptional voice.

Anthony's performance, which gave him his first widespread exposure to non-salsa audiences, began the talk that he was the next Frank Sinatra. Paul Simon was among the first to make the comparison. The talk only increased as people started comparing the two singers. Both Anthony and Sinatra were skinny, ethnic kids from the New York area. Both had dabbled in film. And both had the kind of voice that made women cry and men nod in appreciation.

Involvement in *The Capeman* had delayed Anthony's work on his much anticipated English-language album.

The project was further delayed when he signed on to record the theme song for the movie *The Mask of Zorro*. The holdup, however, only seemed to whet the public's appetite to hear Anthony's next album. The press reported that both Michael Jackson and Eric Clapton thought that Marc Anthony sang like an angel and that Billy Joel couldn't wait to play piano on a future project with Anthony.

"This CD actually deserves the phrase much anticipated," the *Washington Post* wrote before the album was released. "Anthony can sell out arenas on several continents, pack Madison Square Garden and make history with the way his albums fly up Billboard's Latin music charts—but that all barely got noticed by the somewhat insular American mainstream. He's been a salsa singer who records primarily in Spanish, and in this country, in music as in other art forms, you use English if you want to make a serious dent in the culture. Industry insiders and smitten critics have been waiting for the rest of America to discover him."

The self-titled *Marc Anthony* CD was finally released in October 1999. It contained only bits of true salsa, but that didn't seem to matter to listeners. Within days of its release, the first single, "I Need To Know," shot into the Billboard Top Ten. The spirited tune showed flashes of Latin influence, but the remainder of the songs on the album were pop ballads that showcased Anthony's voice at its best. The songs displayed one of Anthony's trademarks—starting a song slowly, even softly, before building to an explosive crescendo in which he seems to hold the notes forever.

Although some worried that hard-core salsa fans would be disappointed by the songs in English, Anthony didn't think so. He pointed out that a lot of his fans were bilingual and would appreciate the English-language album. He also knew that fans would appreciate his passionate singing. Finally, he believed they would understand that singing in English was just another means for Anthony to express himself artistically, not an indication that he was abandoning them.

As if the success of *Marc Anthony* wasn't enough, 1999 also marked a high point in Anthony's acting career. He had already made a small impact in Hollywood with minor roles in such films as 1995's *Hackers*

Anthony might be skinny, but he's got an enormous voice.

(in which he plays a young Secret Service agent) and 1996's *Big Night* (in which he plays a shy kitchen worker). Also in 1996, he appeared as a gangbanger who goes head to head with Tom Berenger in *The Substitute*. Even *The Capeman* fiasco had not been enough to deter Hollywood, which saw something special in the young performer.

Director Martin Scorsese, who like Anthony grew up in a typical New York neighborhood, liked Anthony enough to cast him in his blockbuster *Bringing Out the Dead*. In this film, Anthony plays a homeless man who repeatedly tries to kill himself but keeps getting saved by paramedics, including one played by Nicholas Cage. Despite the involvement of big stars such as Cage, Scorsese told anyone who would listen that Marc Anthony's character was the soul of the movie. Anthony was cast in the role, Scorsese said, because something about him was so sincere.

That sincerity, Anthony says, is an essential part of him. It allows him to feel his songs, to connect with his fans, to stay tied to his fellow Puerto Ricans, and to remain humble about his success and his talent. A perfect example is the relationship Anthony has established with Puerto Rico. Although born in the United States, he has adopted the island as his homeland, and the island has accepted him as a son. So no one was surprised when Anthony announced in 1999 that he wanted to build one hundred homes in Puerto Rico for people who had been left homeless by Hurricane

Looking tough, Marc Anthony played Juan Lacas in The Substitute.

George the year before. To fulfill his promise, Anthony held a series of benefit concerts to raise the estimated $2 million needed for the project. "He is considered something of a saint here," the *New York Times* noted from San Juan, when writing about the relief effort. When Marc married former Miss Universe Dayanara Torres in May 2000, the two decided to share a home in their beloved Puerto Rico.

Anthony also has the patience of a saint, making himself accessible to fans and critics alike. He is humble about his success and is often found wandering around his old neighborhood, joking and laughing with childhood friends. About the only thing that gets him angry these days is being lumped in with other Latino performers who are crossing over from the Spanish to the English mainstream. "I started out singing in English, so what am I crossing over to?" he asks. "That makes it sound like I'm trying my hand at somebody else's music. But I'm just as American as I am Puerto Rican. This is my music as much as anybody else's."

What does the future hold for Marc Anthony? Most everyone agrees that his future is limitless. Unlike many other performers in the Latin pop explosion, he is more artist than performer, which means that his shelf life could be measured not in years but in decades. "Right now, with the impact of world music, he has the whole world in front of him," says his good friend, singer Rubén Blades.

As *Paper Magazine* noted in reviewing an Anthony concert, "Here was this impossibly thin guy with a huge gorgeous voice who sang beautiful songs, sold tons of records, was an actor, had enormous stage presence and was considered a major heartthrob. Now think back awhile: who does that sound like? Will Anthony be known as 'Old Brown Eyes' in a few decades?"

Enrique Iglesias sang a duet with Christina Aguilera at the Super Bowl XXXIV halftime show in January 2000.

Chapter FIVE

ENRIQUE IGLESIAS

ENRIQUE IGLESIAS KNEW VERY EARLY WHAT HE wanted to do with his life. He recalls that, as an eight-year-old, he would kneel in his grandmother's house and pray to be given the chance to sing for a living. As the son of Julio Iglesias, one of the most famous pop crooners in the world, the boy seemed likely to be able to realize his dreams. It would be easy for him to trade in on that fame and follow in his father's footsteps. His father's success would guarantee him at least an audience with record company officials. His last name alone would most likely get him a recording contract, because people would certainly pay to hear the son of Julio Iglesias. After that, his father's influence could probably help him keep working.

Enrique's father, Julio Iglesias, left, sings with feeling.

Everything seemed set for Enrique. All he had to do was ask for it.

But by the time he was a teenager, Enrique had decided that if he was going to succeed he was going to do it on his own. He wanted people to appreciate him for his talent, not his father's. So while his father traveled the world performing romantic ballads for millions of adoring fans, Enrique spent his childhood secretly writing songs and singing in a friend's garage. He was so committed to going it alone that he told none of his relatives about his plans. When he sent out demo tapes of his singing, he did so under an assumed name, telling everyone that he was a struggling singer from Colombia.

"I wanted to be a singer since I was a little kid, but I never told my parents," Enrique said. "I didn't want to hear 'no,' I guess. I didn't want anything negative. It was my thing. If it went right, fine, if it did not, well, why bother? Even now, I have my career very separated from my family. It was the only way I could do it."

Enrique was born on May 8, 1975, in Madrid, Spain, to Spanish pop singer Julio Iglesias and his wife, journalist and socialite Isabel Preysler. Enrique's parents divorced in 1979, and they decided in 1982 that Enrique, his brother, Julio Jr., and their sister,

A young Enrique, right, *has some fun with his family in the pool.*

Chabeli, should live with their paternal grandmother in Miami. Living in the United States would allow the children to learn English, their parents thought. Also, Enrique's grandfather (Julio's father) had been kidnapped by political terrorists in 1981. In Madrid, it seemed, the children would be inviting targets for future attacks. So the kids were shipped off to Miami. "It broke my heart to send them away," said Isabel Preysler. "But we had to for security reasons."

The children were supposed to stay for only a year, but the year stretched into a lifetime as Enrique and the other children settled into Indian Creek, a mansion retreat that Julio Iglesias had built in Miami. While the house was built with every amenity (a pool and tennis courts, for starters), Julio didn't spend much time there. His travel schedule was hectic. And when his father was home, Enrique recalls, the house still did not seem welcoming.

"Sometimes it didn't feel like it was our home," Enrique said. "[The house] felt like it was invaded. Television crews. Businesspeople. It came to the point when there were too many people around the house. I moved out of there when I was ten, to another house nearby. My grandmother was there. And my nanny."

In fact, Enrique focused his love and his attention on his nanny, Elvira Olivares. "She saw me every day," Enrique says. "In a way, she was the closest to being a mother." The two eventually became so close that Enrique dedicated his first album to her.

Enrique hangs out on a boat in the water with his golden retriever.

Living near the beach in Miami, Enrique developed a lifelong love of water and water sports. It continued when he enrolled in high school, where he reports that he was shy and unassuming. So unassuming that he kept getting turned down for dates, including twice for the prom. (Such stories are hard to believe, because Enrique is considered to be one of the sexiest men alive.)

When he was about fifteen, Enrique got serious about singing and making music. Inspired by performers such as Dire Straits, Bob Dylan, Billy Joel,

Fleetwood Mac, and Bruce Springsteen, he spent his afternoons in a basement practicing in secret with friends, composing a variety of songs in both Spanish and English. He even started performing with two older friends in restaurants around Miami's Little Havana neighborhood, so called because of the large number of Cubans living in the area. Although Enrique's voice was strong and full of emotion, he remember that his first few efforts at singing were tough. He thought that both he and the songs were not very good.

Enrique enrolled in the University of Miami as a business administration major, but he couldn't focus much on his studies. "I used to be in math class and [a singing career was] all I used to think about," he said. "When I was at the university, that's all I heard in my mind."

During his freshman year, he finally felt he was polished enough and had enough material to launch his music career. In 1994 he placed a call to Fernan Martinez, who for nine years was Julio Iglesias's publicist and manager. "My first reaction was: He's in trouble," Martinez said. "I thought it was something with a girl, he was so mysterious and secretive! I had no clue."

The reason for the call soon became obvious. Enrique told Martinez that he had dropped out of college to pursue a music career. He then performed a mini-concert for Martinez, singing some songs in English and others in Spanish. That was enough to convince Martinez to sign on as Enrique's manager, although the younger Iglesias insisted on certain conditions. First, Martinez could not tell Enrique's parents what he was doing. Second, he had to tell anyone who heard the demo tape that the singer was named Enrique Martinez and came from Colombia. Finally, under no circumstances could he tell anyone that Enrique was Julio Iglesias's son. "Enrique has always been very proud of his father, really admires him, but he didn't want to be a curiosity," Martinez explained.

Martinez reluctantly agreed to Enrique's demands, wondering how they could pull off such a ruse. But pull it off they did. After being turned down by such record labels as Sony, EMI Latin, and PolyGram Latin America (which thought the music was too simple), Enrique finally signed with Fonovisa, an independent label in Los Angeles. The label paid him the unheard-of sum of one million dollars for three albums, not because of who he was but because of the type of sound he offered.

Although a lot of Spanish-speaking singers were performing at the time—everything from salsa to mariachi songs—almost no young Spanish singers were performing adult contemporary songs. Enrique delivered a modern pop sound, faster and more sophisticated than the traditional Spanish songs and aimed at listeners in their twenties and thirties. "You'd turn on the radio and think what . . . is this," Enrique said of the Spanish music scene when he debuted. "It's great to go back to our roots and to know where Spanish music came from and what it is, but it was people who were dead 20 years ago."

Fonovisa was of the same opinion, and it decided to break the mold and publicize Enrique like no other Latin singer before him. Even before the first album was ready, the company bought millions of dollars in advertising on Spanish-language radio and television stations. It also began buying time on English-language television and arranging for Enrique to appear on such programs as the *Late Show with David Letterman* and the Miss Universe pageant, even though he was not going to be recording in English. Eventually, the marketing campaign became the most expensive in history for a Latino artist.

Enrique's father found out about the record deal at an industry cocktail party, when someone mentioned that he must be quite proud of his son. Julio was shocked and a little upset, not because his son had not told him about his plans, but because Enrique had decided to drop out of school.

Even with the secret out, Enrique remained sensitive about being linked to his father in public. His label advertised him simply as "Enrique." He resisted identifying himself as Julio's son, and he walked out of some media interviews when he was introduced that way. "I didn't want to be introduced as the son of Julio Iglesias," he said. "I wanted to be accepted on my own terms."

The company's faith in Enrique was confirmed in September 1995 with the release of Enrique's first album, *Enrique Iglesias*. Almost immediately, the first single, "Si Tú Te Vas" (If You Go), shot to number one on the Billboard Latin charts, selling more than five million copies. Four songs from the album would reach number one. It wasn't long before people were calling Enrique "the Elvis of Latin America."

Like Elvis Presley, Enrique was very much the showman. During concerts, he usually selected a young woman from the audience and brought her onstage to

Enrique woos the crowd.

serenade her. Record sales proved his reputation as he became the best-selling Latin performer in the world.

He issued his second album, *Vivir* (To Live), to even greater success in 1997. This album also spawned several number-one songs. By the time his third album, *Cosas del Amor* (Things of Love), was released in 1998, he had stretched his string of number-one hits to a remarkable ten in a row while selling more than fourteen million albums. Along the way, he won a Grammy Award in 1997 for best Latin pop performance.

"When Enrique first came out, we thought that he would rise on the basis of his name alone," said Fernando Jaramillo, music director of WOJO-FM in Chicago. "But when we paid close attention to him, we discovered that he had a lot of talent and that was what was making him go to the top of the charts. Not because he was the son of Julio Iglesias."

Still, Enrique could never completely avoid the long shadow cast by his famous father. "It's pathetic," Enrique said. "Even after I won the Grammy, I heard this girl say, 'Oh, you won a Grammy because your dad is Julio Iglesias' and you know the funny thing is that last year my father was nominated for a Grammy and he didn't win. I don't like to get into it but I'm tired of hearing 'Do you think you sell more records because of your dad?' Well, right now in the U.S. I sell more records than my father. So it would seem a little contradictory that people are buying the records only for who my dad is."

It seemed that if Enrique was finally going to get away from his father's legacy, he would have to do something spectacular. And Enrique thought he knew just what to do—cross over into English and conquer the mainstream pop music audience in the United States. Like many of his contemporaries, including Ricky Martin and Marc Anthony, Enrique wanted to sing in English to appeal to a wider audience. Enrique had already recorded in three languages (Italian, Portuguese, and Spanish), but he knew that English held the key to his career.

Early in 1999, Ricky Martin had set the Grammy Awards on fire. Actor/comedian/singer Will Smith and other music-industry power brokers were quick to notice and to figure out that Latino performers, and Latin-flavored music, could be big in 1999. So Enrique got a great career boost when Smith asked him to contribute a song to the soundtrack of the 1999 summer movie *The Wild Wild West.*

What a song it proved to be. "Bailamos" debuted at number one when it was released that summer. It became an anthem of sorts, selected as the introductory music for boxer Oscar De La Hoya's big fight with Ike Quartey in Las Vegas. The song, included on Enrique's first English-language album, *Enrique,* eventually sold more than one million copies, going platinum before the fall of 1999. Suddenly, it seemed, people all over the world began thinking of Julio Iglesias not as a famous crooner but as the father of *Enrique* Iglesias.

Does Enrique Iglesias have the staying power to compete in the world of pop music for years to come?

The elder Iglesias, who has sold more than one hundred million records himself, says he is very proud of his son's success. "I think it is amazing," Julio said. "He is an amazing kid. He has a lot of class, a lot of charm, a lot of talent. Sometimes I look at him and I don't believe this guy is so young and so successful."

Julio can take credit for some of that success. Although Enrique has distanced himself from his father's professional life, he is quick to admit that he has learned valuable lessons from his father. Having grown up in the limelight surrounding Julio, Enrique is incredibly comfortable being famous. He also learned a lot about the business of music by watching Julio handle his multimillion-dollar empire. Finally, observing Julio has helped Enrique handle his own fame.

"I am not impressed by money or fame," says Enrique. "I've been lucky. I grew up around that. I knew that if I failed I would always have something to eat. And in terms of fame and adulation I have grown up around my father. I've seen it up close, and I've learned a lot. Some people think because of that I would be even more egotistical, and it's exactly the opposite. That's my advantage. I assure you that if what had happened to me this past year had happened to a twenty-one-year-old kid who's had nothing, it would have destroyed him psychologically."

Julio's career has been long and varied. As a result of watching his father's ups and downs, Enrique says he has learned that musical tastes and popularity, especially in the United States, can be fleeting things. "It's tough," he says. "One year you're hot and the next year you're cold. And the hotter you were, the colder you get. Haven't you seen VH1's [television program] *Where Are They Now?* I mean it's scary to see the guy that was huge 10 years ago saying, 'Yeah, I'm gonna be back,' as he's gardening in his yard." Enrique sums up, "That's one show I don't want to be on."

Many people consider Gloria Estefan, shown with her husband, Emilio, *and the Miami Sound Machine to be the first successful crossover band in U.S. music-industry history.*

CONCLUSION

It is with good reason that Emilio Estefan is called "the Godfather of Latin Pop." From his home in Miami, Emilio has helped his Cuban wife, Gloria Estefan, become the most successful Latin singer in the United States. Singing in English and Spanish in the 1970s, Gloria Estefan and the Miami Sound Machine created a unique musical style that combined fast-paced tropical Latin sounds with traditional pop rhythms.

The music proved an immense success, leading in the 1980s to the sale of more than seventy million albums. Although the Miami Sound Machine created quite a stir, Emilio and Gloria were unable to create the type of hysteria over Latin music that greeted such performers as Ricky Martin, Jennifer Lopez, and Enrique Iglesias in 1999. Emilio Estefan thinks that mainstream fans and the music industry were not yet ready for his band's music because the sound and rhythms were still so foreign to many listeners.

With so many Latino acts crossing into the English-speaking mainstream, Estefan believes that Latino performers will be able to sustain their success. In fact, he is banking on it. Emilio spends a lot of his time in his Crescent Moon Studios—producing, recording, and establishing members of the next generation of Latino artists. He has been joined in this commitment by major record labels. The record companies are more willing to take a chance (and spend money) on new Latino talent these days, another significant switch from when the Estefans started out.

"Gloria and I went through the hardest part," Emilio said. "A dozen years ago, a label threw me out when I tried to use congas on a recording. They said, 'Get rid of that, and take out the horns and the timbales, too.' Now people are buying records by Arturo Sándoval and Buena Vista Social Club. The younger generation is now reacting to Latin music."

Many of Cuba's finest singers and musicians came together to tour as a group called the Buena Vista Social Club.

Estefan believes that the new widespread acceptance of Latino music bodes well for the singers he is developing. His optimism is fueled by some amazing numbers. In the next ten to twenty years, Latinos are expected to overtake African Americans to become the largest minority group in the United States. And the buying power of Latinos is expected to increase from about $300 billion at the turn of the century to more than $500 billion by the year 2020.

And a lot of that money is being spent on music and entertainment. In 1997 Latin music sales totaled about $490 million, according to the Record Industry Artist Association. By 1998 that figure had grown to more than $570 million, with prospects of more than $600 million in sales in 1999.

"The whole Latin music phenomenon shows no signs of slowing down and every sign that it's going to be with us for a long, long time," observed television journalist José Diaz-Balart. "This is not the first time that Latin artists have influenced American music, nor is it the first time that a male pop star has mesmerized the nation's females with his hips, but it is undoubtedly [the first time] that Latin pop has sat so high on top of the music world and drawn so much attention from Anglo listeners."

Further proof of the underlying strength of the Latino music explosion is the fact that influential English-language performers are willing to make Latin music "the Next Big Thing." Musicians ranging from

As Latino and crossover artists become more and more popular, they pave the way for up-and-coming singers like Shakira, right.

Madonna to Will Smith to Sean "Puffy" Combs have stampeded to get in on the action. And some English-language acts are even doing a sort of reverse crossover, seeking to take a bite out of the growing Latino market. For instance, when Combs released his latest single, "PE 2000," he also released a Spanish-language version of the work. He filmed the video for the song at New York's annual Puerto Rican Day parade, which attracts more than two million people each year.

"Latino people have a golden key in their hands, a common treasure," said Shakira, a twenty-two-year-old Colombian singer whom the Estefans and others believe could be the next big crossover star. "That treasure is fusion. The fusion of rhythm, the fusion of ideas. We Latinos are a race of fusion, that is the music we make. And so at the dawn of a new millennium, when everything is said and done, what could possibly happen besides a fusion?"

In essence, what is happening is the maturation of the Latino community in the United States as it works to reach its potential in business, sports, and entertainment. The leading agents of change are the entertainers, because of their ability to influence the youngest members of society. And many Latino entertainers realize the significance of the roles they are playing.

"It's important for Latinos everywhere," Enrique Iglesias said about the growing popularity of Latino artists. "You're not presenting [non-Latino audiences] with a solo singer. You're presenting them with a whole different culture, a whole different race. It's great."

SOURCES

8   Guy Garcia, "Jennifer Lopez Is Moving Latin Music,"
    Patriot Ledger, (July 2, 1999), 19.

9   Christopher John Farley, "Latin Music Goes Pop," *Time,*
    (May 24, 1999), 74.

11 Lydia Martin, "Selena's Husband Strives to Move On,"
    Orlando Sentinel, (August 18, 1999), E-2.

14 Joey Guerra, "Border Music," *Houston Chronicle,* (June
    13, 1999), 8.

16 Rick Mitchell, "Selena," *Houston Chronicle,* (May 21, 1995), 6.

17 Ibid.

19 Ibid.

19 Abraham Quintanilla, liner notes, *Selena Anthology,* EMI
    Latin and Q Productions, 1998.

23 Ibid.

24 Mitchell, 6.

24 Ibid.

27 Suzanne Lopez Medina, "Selena's Star Still Shines,"
    Arizona Republic, (March 31, 1996), A-1.

27–28 Quintanilla.

29 Guerra, 8.

29 Alisa Valdes-Rodriguez, "Pop Music," *Los Angeles Times,*
    (May 9, 1999), 3.

30 Lopez Medina, A-1.

31 *Latinolink,* March 20, 1997, <http://www.latinolink.com>
    (n.d.)

34–35 Jeremy Helligar, "Ricky Martin," *Teen People,* (September
    1999), 12.

36 Nancy Wilson, *CBC Infoculture,* June 29, 1999,
    <http://www.infoculture.com> (September 3, 1999).

38–39 Namrata Bhawnani, *Reddiff on the Net,* June 20, 1998,
    <http://www.rediff.com> (August 25, 1999).

39 Farley, 74.

42 Wilson.

43 *BBC Online Network,* July 12, 1999, <http://news/bbc.co.uk/
    hi/english/entertainment/newisd> (September 3, 1999).

45 John Lannert, "Latin Music Is No Passing Fancy," *Billboard*, (September 18, 1999), 1.

45 Nancy Collins, "Ricky Martin: The Rolling Stone Interview," *Rolling Stone*, (August 6, 1999), 50.

45 Jeffrey Zaslow, "Do One Thing at a Time and Do It Right," *USA Weekend*, (November 5–7, 1999), 13.

45 Helligar, 13.

48 Garcia, 19.

50 Paige Smoron, "La Vida Lopez," *Chicago Sun Times*, (September 26, 1999), 14.

50 Dennis Duggan, "A Rising Latina Star Wows Them in the Bronx," *Newsday*, (March 20, 1999), A-4.

56–57 Ibid.

57 Julian Ives, *Mr. Showbiz*, n.d., <http://Mrshowbiz.go.com/people/jenniferlopez> (n.d.).

57 Ed Morales, "It's Not La Vida Loca to Her," *Los Angeles Times*, (May 5, 1999), 4.

58 Veronica Chambers and John Leland, "Lovin' La Vida Loca," *Newsweek*, (May 31, 1999), 73–74.

58 Kelvin Tong, "Dangerous Curves," *The Straight Times* (Singapore), (October 1998), L-1.

59 Dream Hampton, "Boomin' System," *Vibe*, (August 1999), 104.

60 Elysa Gardner, "She's All That," *InStyle*, (June 1, 1999), 276.

61 Rush & Malloy, "Puffy Has a Proposal for Jennifer," *New York Daily News*, November 7, 1999, <http://www.nydailynews.com/1999-11-07/News_and_Views/Daily_Dish/a-46452.asp> (May 22, 2000).

63 Daniel Chang, "Hot Latin Crossover Acts," *Fort Worth Star-Telegram*, (May 30, 1999), 6.

63 Garcia, 19.

65 Alisa Valdes, "Salsa's New Voice," *Boston Globe*, (December 13, 1996), D17.

66 Chiqui Cartagena, "Marc Gets Set," *New York Daily News*, (September 20, 1998), <http://www.nydailynews.com/1998-09-20/New_York_Now/Music/a-5530.asp> (May 22, 2000).

67 Chris Willman, "Marquee Marc," *Entertainment Weekly*, (October 8, 1999), 34.

67 *La Musica.com,* July 1, 1996, <http://www.lamusica.com/marcaol.htm> (October 11, 1999).

72 Robert Dominguez, "The Marc of Capeman," *New York Daily News,* (January 1, 1998), 24.

73 Valdes, D17.

74–75 Daisann McLane, "The Voice of the New Salsa," *Village Voice,* (October 1997), 1.

75–76 Willman, 34.

77 Elysa Gardner, "Not Just Another Latin Sensation," *USA Today,* (October 4, 1999), 4-D.

79 Paula Span, "Hotter Than Salsa," *Washington Post,* (October 5, 1999), C-1.

82 Stephen J. Dubner, "Ricky Who?" *New York Times,* (August 29, 1999), 42.

83 Willman, 34.

83 Ibid.

83 Anita Sarko, "El Niño," *Paper Magazine,* (April 1998), (n.p.).

87 Fernando Gonzalez, "A Famous Son Takes His Place at the Top of Pop," *The Record* (Northern New Jersey) (December 31, 1996), 1.

88 Peter Castro, "On the Move," *People,* (April 22, 1996), 144.

88 "The Clan with a Tan," *The Observer,* (July 11, 1999), (accessed via the Dow Jones interactive, fee-based, members-only Website at <http://nrstg1p.djnr.com>).

88 Ibid.

90 Ernesto Portillo Jr., "Young Man in a Hurry," *San Diego Union-Tribune,* (March 4, 1999), Night & Day section, 4.

90 Richard Harrington, "The Son Is Very Hot," *Washington Post,* (January 28, 1999), C-1.

91 Ramiro Burr, "The Son Also Rises," *San Antonio Express News,* (April 9, 1999), 1-H.

91–92 Harrington, C-1.

92 Burr, 1-H.

94 Monica Eng, "The Son Also Rises," *Chicago Tribune,* (June 1, 1997), 12.

94 Ibid.

96 Ibid.

97 Fernando Gonzalez, "Julio? Isn't He Enrique Iglesias' Father?" *Buffalo News,* (December 1, 1996), E-1.

97   Betty Cortina, "Enrique Suave for Years," *Entertainment Weekly*, (November 26, 1999), 56.
100   Farley, 74.
101   Jose Diaz-Balart, "Latin Music Bursts Into Pop Culture," *CBS News: This Morning*, (June 14, 1999).
102–3 Farley, 74.
103   Ernesto Portilla Jr., Night & Day section, 4.

SELECTED BIBLIOGRAPHY

Castro, Peter. "On the Move." *People*, April 22, 1996.

Chambers, Veronica, and John Leland. "Lovin' La Vida Loca." *Newsweek*, May 31, 1999.

Collins, Nancy. "Ricky Martin: The Rolling Stone Interview." *Rolling Stone*, August 6, 1999.

Cortina, Betty. "Enrique Suave for Years." *Entertainment Weekly*, November 26, 1999.

Farley, Christopher John. "Latin Music Goes Pop." *Time*, May 24, 1999.

Gardner, Elysa. "She's All That." *InStyle*, June 1, 1999.

Hampton, Dream. "Boomin' System." *Vibe*, August 1999.

Helligar, Jeremy. "Ricky Martin." *Teen People*, September 1999.

Lannert, John. "Latin Music Is No Passing Fancy." *Billboard*, September 18, 1999.

Sarko, Anita. "El Niño." *Paper Magazine*, April 1998.

——. "Marc Anthony." *Interview*, February 1, 1999.

SELECTED DISCOGRAPHY

SELENA

16 Super Éxitos Originales (16 Greatest Original Hits) (1990, EMI Latin)

Ven Conmigo (Come with Me) (1990, EMI Latin)

Entertainers of the Year (1992)
Entre a Mi Mundo (Come into My World) (1992, EMI Latin)
Live (1993, EMI Latin. Recorded at El Coleseo Memorial in
    Corpus Christi, TX, February 7, 1993)
Mis Mejores Canciones: 17 Super Exitos (My Best Songs: 17
    Greatest Hits) (1993, EMI Latin)
Amor Prohibido (1994, EMI Latin)
12 Super Éxitos (12 Greatest Hits) (1994, EMI Latin)

RICKY MARTIN
Ricky Martin (1991, Sony Discos, Inc.)
Me Amarás (1993, Sony Discos, Inc.)
A Medio Vivir (1995, Sony Discos, Inc.)
Vuelve (1998, Sony Discos, Inc.)
Ricky Martin (1999, C2 Records)

JENNIFER LOPEZ
On the 6 (1999, Work Group)

MARC ANTHONY
Otra Nota (1993, re-released in 1999 by Sony Discos, Inc.)
Toda a Su Tiempo (1995, re-released in 1999 by Sony Discos,
    Inc.)
Contra la Corriente (1997, re-released in 1999 by Sony Discos,
    Inc.)
Desde un Principio/From the Beginning (1999, Sony Discos, Inc.
    A compilation album)
Marc Anthony (1999, re-released in 1999 by Sony Discos, Inc.)

ENRIQUE IGLESIAS
Enrique Iglesias (1995, Fonovisa)
Vivir (1997, Fonovisa)
Cosas del Amor (1998, Fonovisa)
Bailamos (greatest hits album, 1999, Fonovisa)
Enrique (1999, Interscope Records)
The Best Hits (2000, Fonovisa)

INDEX

OTHER TITLES FROM LERNER AND A&E®:

Arthur Ashe
Bill Gates
Bruce Lee
Carl Sagan
Chief Crazy Horse
Christopher Reeve
Edgar Allan Poe
Eleanor Roosevelt
George Lucas
Gloria Estefan
Jack London
Jacques Cousteau
Jane Austen
Jesse Owens
Jesse Ventura
Jimi Hendrix
John Glenn
Legends of Dracula

Legends of Santa Claus
Louisa May Alcott
Madeleine Albright
Mark Twain
Maya Angelou
Mohandas Gandhi
Mother Teresa
Nelson Mandela
Princess Diana
Queen Cleopatra
Queen Latifah
Rosie O'Donnell
Saint Joan of Arc
Thurgood Marshall
Wilma Rudolph
Women in Space
Women of the Wild West

ABOUT THE AUTHOR

Herón Márquez, born in Mexico, moved to California at the age of six. After a short career playing semiprofessional baseball, he took up writing. He has worked as a journalist for such papers as the *Albuquerque Journal, New York Daily News, Los Angeles Times, Santa Barbara News Press,* and the *Minneapolis Star Tribune.* Márquez lives in St. Paul, Minnesota, with his wife Traecy.

PHOTO ACKNOWLEDGMENTS

Retna, Ltd.: (© Morrison Wulffraat) p. 2, (© Larry Busacca) p. 12, (© Kelly Swift) p. 35, (© E. Paniccioli) p. 38, (© Neal Preston) p. 41, (© Steve Granitz) p. 42, (© David Atlas) p. 44, (© Walter McBride) p. 78, (© Stills) p. 87, (© Scott Teittler) pp. 89, 96, (© John Kelly) p. 93; Liaison Agency, Inc.: (© Benainous/Scorcelletti) p. 6, (© David Adame) p. 26, (© Tom Fox) pp. 22, 27, 30, (© Lawrence Schwartzwald) pp. 61, 74, (© Christian Ducasse) p. 71; Everett Collection, pp. 10, 31, 51, 53, 55, 56, 68, 86; Archive Photos: (Reuters/Pool) p. 20, (Manny Hernandez) p. 21, (Reuters/Colin Braley) p. 32, (Frank Driggs) p. 37, (Reuters/Fred Prouser) p. 46, (Reuters/Sam Mircovich) p. 49, (Victor Malafronte) p. 59, (Reuters/Rose Prouser) p. 62, (Alberto Tamargo) p. 98; Globe Photos, Inc.: (© S. Moskowitz) p. 15, (© Lisa Rose) p. 28, (© Andrea Renault) p. 34, (© Bara Nemser) p. 80, (© Alan Markfield) p. 82; Classmates.com Yearbook Archives, p. 52; Corbis: (© AFP) pp. 64, 84, 102, (© Reuters Newmedia, Inc.) p. 100. Cover photos
Hardcover: front, © Zach Corder/Latin Focus.com (far left); Everett Collection (upper left); © Benainous/Scorcelletti/Liaison Agency, Inc. (upper right); © Fitzroy Barrett/Globe Photos, Inc. (lower right); © Scorcelletti/Vandeville/Liaison Agency, Inc. (lower left); back, © Steve Granitz/Retna, Ltd.
Softcover: front, Reuters/Jeff Christensen/Archive Photos; back, © AFP/Corbis